Three Little Sheep

For
Steve, Sue and Alexander Walters

Published in Wales in 2010 by Pont Books, an imprint of
Gomer Press, Llandysul, Ceredigion, SA44 4JL

ISBN 978 1 84851 155 2

A CIP record for this title is available from the British Library.

This book is published with the financial support of the
Welsh Books Council.

Printed and bound in Wales at
Gomer Press, Llandysul, Ceredigion

Three Little Sheep

Rob Lewis

Pont

Three little sheep went out one day
Into the meadow to run and play.

Olwen skipped in the field for hours
While Meg and Flo explored the flowers.

Then on the breeze they heard a sound.
It seemed to come from a hole in the ground.
Deep in the darkness, loud and strong,
Someone below was singing a song.

'I wonder,' said Meg, 'who lives in that hole?
Perhaps it's a miner digging for coal.'

'Ssh!' said Flo. 'Don't make a sound.
We need to know who is underground.'
She leaned too far and in fell a stone
Then far below they heard a groan.
Whoever it was stopped singing his song.

And up popped a wolf, saying, 'What's going on?'

'Quick!' said Olwen. 'We must flee.
The wolf will eat us up for tea!'
'It's safe in the trees, I'm sure,' said Flo.
'That is a place no wolf will go.'
They ran and ran as fast as they could,
Across the meadow and into a wood.

'The wolf has gone,'
said Meg at last.
'Let's go back home
now the danger's past.'

Then tramp, tramp, tramp, singing his song,
They saw the wolf come following on . . .

'Here's a place no wolf can go.
It's safe in here, I'm sure,' said Flo.
'There's no way that a wolf will see
If we hide in the trunk of this
rotten tree.'

They hid inside.
It was quite a squeeze,
But the tree was home
to a swarm of bees.

They left the furious bees behind,
But turning around, what did
they find?

Tramp, tramp, tramp, singing his song,
Still the wolf came following on . . .

They hurried along to a fast-flowing river.

The rushing water made them quiver.

'Here's a place no wolf will go.

It's safe to cross, I'm sure,' said Flo.

'There's no way that a wolf can swim.

The water's far too cold for him.'

They managed to cross though the river was wide
But they got a surprise on the other side.
None of the sheep had noticed a bridge
Hidden behind a grassy ridge.

Tramp, tramp, tramp, singing his song,
Still the wolf came following on . . .

The journey soon turned hard and steep.
The friends were tired. They wanted to sleep.
'This is a place no wolf will go.
It's safe up here, I'm sure,' said Flo.
'There's no way that a wolf can cope
With climbing up such a rocky slope.'
They clambered on and did not stop,
Till, cut and bruised, they reached the top.

But looking around, they got a shock
When the wolf appeared from behind
a rock.

Tramp, tramp, tramp, singing his song,
Still the wolf came following on . . .

Over the hills the three sheep went
Till almost all of their strength was spent.
'Here's a place no wolf can go.
It's safe in here, I'm sure,' said Flo.
'There's no way that a wolf can catch
Sheep in the middle of a bramble patch.'
They fought their way through prickle and thorn
Until their wool was ragged and torn.

A snipping sound then reached their ears.
Someone was coming with a pair of shears!

Snip, snip, snip, singing his song,
Still the wolf came following on.

Then they came to a field of sludge.
Through the mud they started to trudge.
'Here's a place no wolf will go.
I'm sure we're safe in here,' said Flo.
'There's no way that the wolf will chase
Three little sheep through this boggy place.'
They slipped and slid and were nearly stuck,
Till all three sheep were covered in muck.

But squish, squish, squish, singing his song,
Still the wolf came following on.

Through the fields they wearily toiled,
Battered and bruised with wool all soiled.
At last they came to their own sheep shed.
'We're home! Let's get inside!' they said.

'We're safe in here,' said Flo, 'I'm sure,'
As they hurried inside and barred the door.

But the wolf, he wandered round the shack
Until he spotted a hole at the back . . .

It was dark in the shed but there seemed to be
Four pairs of eyes instead of three!

Then the three little sheep had a terrible fright.
'Hello!' said the wolf, as he turned on the light.

'I followed you home. I hope you don't mind,
But I think you left these ribbons behind.'
All three sheep were so relieved,
The wolf was not what they believed.
This friendly wolf was kind and good.
They wanted to thank him if they could.

So the wolf stayed for tea and shared some cake,

While Flo explained their big mistake.

The wolf laughed loudly. Then he said,

'It's time for me to go to bed.

But I like the way that our story ends:

Now three little sheep and a wolf are friends.'

Then he waved goodbye, saying, 'See you soon,'
And he set off home by the light of the moon.

And over the hill, loud and strong,
Came the sound of the wolf still singing his song . . .